BUFFALO SNOW

By Elizabeth Leader and Eve Tulbert

ISBN: 978-1-4243-2471-2

Distributed by Western New York Wares, Inc.
P.O. Box 733
Ellicott Station
Buffalo, New York 14205
(716) 832-6088
www.buffalobooks.com

Printed by Petit Printing
155 Rano Street
Buffalo, New York 14207

Dedicated to

Buffalo, New York

The City of Good Neighbors

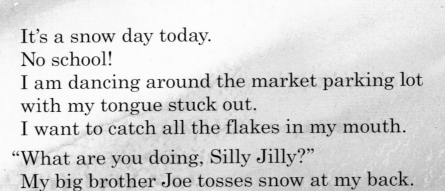

It's a snow day today.
No school!
I am dancing around the market parking lot
with my tongue stuck out.
I want to catch all the flakes in my mouth.

"What are you doing, Silly Jilly?"
My big brother Joe tosses snow at my back.

"You're mean!" I stick my tongue out and run.
I make a snowball between my hands.
I'm gonna throw it at him
when he turns around.

"Come on, Jill. Let's get the groceries."
My brother's face is worried.
He just learned to drive.

"Are you afraid?" I say.

"Let's just get home before the
storm comes."

"When's it coming?" I say.

"Today," he says. "Sometime today.
Let's hurry up."

I'm looking at the grocery bags in the car.
"Did you get marshmallows, Joe?"

"Maybe so."

"Hot chocolate?"

"In my pocket."

"Are you gonna share?"

"Do you care?"

"I hate it when you rhyme me, Joe!"

"Wow, there's a whole lot of snow."

Suddenly, wind blows hard against the car.
Snow is everywhere.
The sidewalk disappears.
The people disappear.
The streetlights disappear.
And the cars around us, they all disappear.
I hold my hands out in front of me
To make sure I don't disappear.
The car stops moving.

"Joe! What's happening?"

"It's a blizzard, Jilly."

"A blizzard?"

"Just sit tight. We'll be fine. The snow plow
will come, and we'll get home."

I know he's afraid because his
mouth makes a frown.
He's wiping off the window with his gloves.
He's trying to see something.
We wait a long, long time.
Wind is shaking the car.

"I'm so cold, Joe."

"We've got to get out of this car, Jilly.
We've got to get somewhere warm."

"Okay," I say. Now I'm really afraid.

"You've got to hold on tight to my jacket.
Don't let go."

We are walking. It's so cold.
I lift my feet up high. Snow is in my boots.
I remember the hot chocolate in the car.
"Joe, did you take the marshmallows?"

"No, Jilly, don't worry about the marshmallows."

"There's snow in my socks, Joe."

"Just keep walking, Jilly.
We'll be home soon." But we're far from home.
I know we're far from home.

We see a house through the snow.
There are lights in the windows.
Joe pulls me up steps.
He pulls my arm too hard.
"Come on, Jill."

Joe knocks hard on the door.
A lady answers. "Oh, my!"

"Our car is stuck," says Joe,
"Can we use your phone?"

"Come on in – you must be frozen!"

I hear a little girl's voice.
"Are they snowmen, Mama?"

The lady takes off my coat
and she wraps me up in a blanket.
The little girl holds my hands in her hands.
"Your fingers are like icicles," she says.
Her name is Keisha.

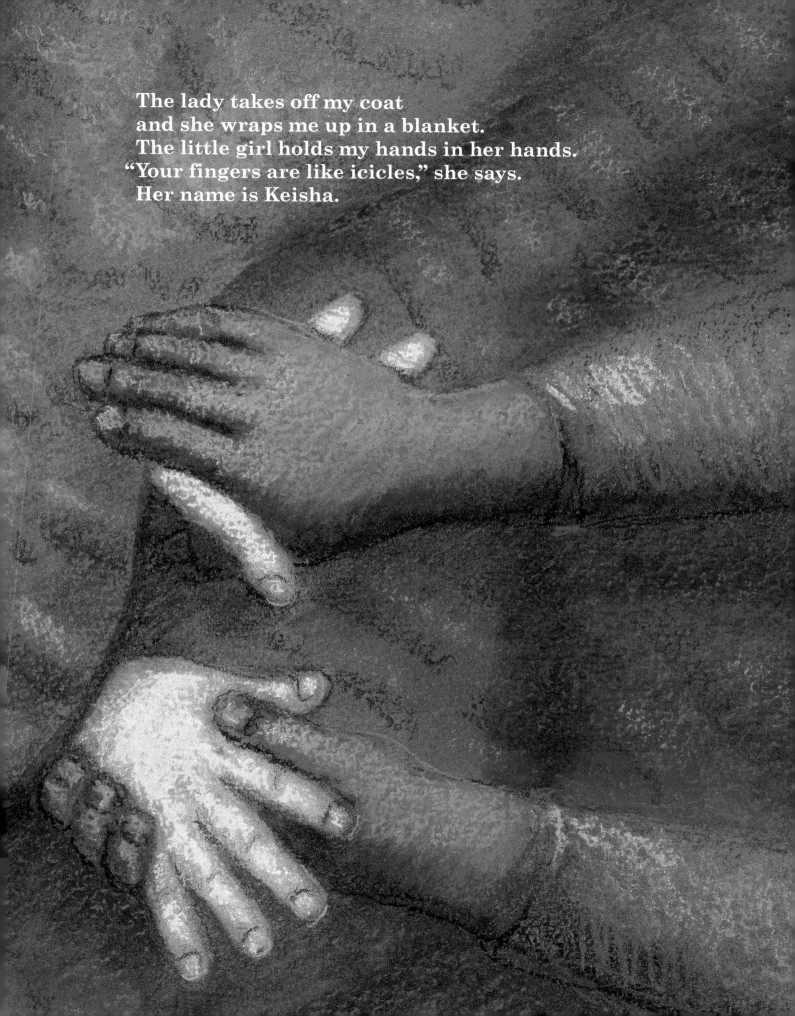

I hear Joe. He's trying to call on the phone.
"You just have to wait here 'til the snow stops,"
says Keisha's mom, Mrs. Johnson.
But the snow is everywhere. It won't stop.
The wind keeps shaking the windows.

"My dad is stuck at work," says Keisha.
"He's going to have to sleep under his desk."

"When will we see Mom and Daddy, Joe?"

"I'm not sure where they are," says Joe.
"I've left three messages on the answering machine."

"Don't cry," says Keisha. "Don't cry."

Mrs. Johnson gives us bowls
of macaroni and cheese.
Joe eats like a monster.
Mrs. Johnson refills our bowls.
"Would you like a cup of
hot chocolate?" she says.
I look at Joe and grin.

"My sister can't have any.
She's allergic."

"It's not true," I shout.

"Are you allergic to
marshmallows?"

"Yes," says Joe.

"**NO**," I say.

Keisha puts three big
marshmallows in my cup.
It is delicious!

Mrs. Johnson and Joe watch TV news.
"This is the biggest storm we've had in years," she says.

Keisha and I are too busy for TV. We put on old hats
from her closet. She sings, "Show me how to get down,"
and we jump on her bed. She can do a flip, and I can do
high kicks in the air.

Mrs. Johnson shouts,
"Show's over.
It's time for bed."
We take off the hats.
We get under the
warm covers.

Joe comes in and says,
"Good night, Jilly.
We'll see Mom and Dad
in the morning."

But I can't sleep.

I am watching the snow falling
past the window.
Everything is covered in white.
Everything glows in the rays
of the streetlight.
Where does this much snow come from?
I wonder.
All I can hear is the wind roaring above me.
All night I keep waking up.
"When will Mom and Daddy come?"

Keisha wakes up and tells me, "Don't worry."
She shows me the crystals on the window.
"They're beautiful diamonds," she says.

The wind is shaking the roof.
In my dream, I see a herd of white buffalo.
They are running over the roof.
They are stampeding in the streets.
They are stamping in the snow.
They leave their hoofprints.
I dream that Mom and Daddy follow
the buffalo's hoofprints so they
can find us again.

Knock, knock, knock!

A loud knock on the door wakes me up in the morning.

It's Daddy! I run down the stairs.

Keisha shouts, "Woohooo!"

Daddy swings me up in a big circle then pounds Joe on the back.

We put on our coats, and they are warm and dry. Outside, the sky is bright blue. Daddy and Joe shovel out Mrs. Johnson's driveway.

"Keisha, look here!" I shout. "It's the buffalo prints. It wasn't a dream!"

We bend over to look and Joe hits me with a snowball. I just laugh. Keisha and I roll over and make angels in the snow.

"Are you ready to go?" says Daddy.

First I have to hug Mrs. Johnson.
Then I sing a song with Keisha.
We do a special friends handshake.
Then I am ready to go home.